# Danny's Sick Trick

WITHDRAWN

FROM STOCK

Brianóg Brady Dawson
• Pictures by Michael Connor •

℗Ɓ
THE O'BRIEN PRESS
DUBLIN

First published 2000 by The O'Brien Press Ltd,
20 Victoria Road, Dublin 6, Ireland.
Tel: +353 1 4923333; Fax: +353 1 4922777
E-mail: books@obrien.ie
Website: www.obrien.ie
Reprinted 2002, 2003.

ISBN: 0-86278-689-4

British Library Cataloguing-in-Publication Data
Dawson, Brianog Brady
Danny's sick trick. - (O'Brien pandas ; 15)
1.Children's stories
I.Title II.Connor, Michael
823.9'14[J]

3  4  5  6  7  8  9  10
03  04  05  06  07  08

Typesetting, layout, editing, design: The O'Brien Press Ltd
Printing: Cox & Wyman Ltd

For Claire and Katie, with love

Can YOU spot the panda
hidden in the story?

Mum and Dad were ready.
Little Susie was ready.
But Danny wasn't ready.

'I'm not going to
Auntie Bessie's house!'
he yelled. 'No way!'

Dad got cross.

'Auntie Bessie and Uncle Tom
have invited us to see
their new house,' he said.
'And you're going!'

'Now, get your runners on,'
said Mum.
'Fast!'

Danny thought of a trick.

His runners were beside his bed.

He quickly kicked them
under the bed.

'I can't find my runners,'
he shouted.
'We'll have to go
to Auntie Bessie's another day.'

Mum stuck her head around
the bedroom door.

'Wear your other shoes,
Danny,' she said.
'The nice, shiny black ones.'

'Never!' said Danny.
He dived under the bed
and fished out his runners.
'I found them!' he cried.

Danny's runners were
very dirty. He wiped them
on his jumper.

Susie was watching him.
She was putting her teddy
on her new pink potty.

Danny grabbed Susie's teddy.
He hid it in the wardrobe.

Susie began to scream.
'**Waaaaaaaaaaaaaaah**.'

'What's wrong now?'
yelled Dad.

'Susie can't find her teddy,'
said Danny.
Susie cried and cried.

'Mum says we can
never go **anywhere**
without that teddy!'
said Danny.

'**Waaaaaaaaaaaaah**!'
cried Susie,
louder than ever.

'You and Mum can go
to Auntie Bessie's,'
said Danny.
'I'll mind Susie.'

Dad looked under Danny's bed.
He looked in
Danny's schoolbag.
Then he looked
in the wardrobe.

He found Susie's teddy.
'No more tricks, Danny,'
he said. 'Now, hurry up
or we'll be late for dinner.'

'**Dinner**?' cried Danny.
He almost fell into
the pink potty!
'Not dinner! We're not going
to Auntie Bessie's for
our dinner! **Oh no**!'

Auntie Bessie was
a terrible cook!
The smells in her kitchen
were awful.
She liked to cook
**pigs' feet
and cabbage**.

'I'm not hungry,'
said Danny.
'You go. I'll mind
the house.'

Mum and Dad were
not listening.
They were talking about
how to get to Auntie Bessie's
new house.

'I've drawn a map,' said Mum.
'It's in the car.'

'Danny,' said Dad,
'you take Susie to the car
while we lock up.'

Danny sat in the car with Susie.

He was feeling very cross.

Mum and Dad were
locking up the house.
The map was lying on
Mum's seat.

If we didn't have that stupid
map, thought Danny,
we'd never find
Auntie Bessie's new house.

Then Danny had
a wonderful idea!

He grabbed the map.
He tore it into bits.

He tore the bits
into smaller bits.
Susie laughed.

Just then, Danny saw
Mum and Dad coming.
He began to pick up
the bits of the map.

'If Mum and Dad see these,'
he said, 'I'm in
**big trouble**!'

Danny looked around
for somewhere to hide the bits.

Sometimes he put his rubbish
down the back of his seat.
Mum and Dad never
looked in there.

They were getting nearer.
Danny picked up
some of the bits.
He pushed them
down the back of his seat.

Mum was at the car door
and Danny still had
some of the map
in his hand.

Mum opened the car door.

Quick as a flash,

Danny stuffed the rest of map

**into his mouth**.

Mum searched for the map.
She looked on her seat.
She looked in her bag.
She couldn't find it.

'We'll have to ring
Auntie Bessie again,'
said Mum.

Mum and Dad went back
into the house.

Danny spat out the map.
Susie started spitting too.
'It's not funny!' said Danny.
'My trick is not working.'

Danny thought of dinner.
'I can nearly smell that
cabbage!' he groaned.
'And it smells sick!
Sick! **Sick! Sick**!'

Then Danny had
another great idea.

He put his hand down
the back of the seat.
He could feel stale crisps.

He could feel an old apple core.

He could feel
Susie's broken biscuits.

'I could eat all this rubbish,
Susie,' said Danny.
'That would make me
**really sick**!
Then I couldn't go
to Auntie Bessie's house!'
Danny smiled to himself
and reached down.

He put some of the rubbish
into his mouth.

It tasted awful.
'**Yuck**!' said Danny.
'Yuck! Yuck!' said Susie.

Mum and Dad jumped
back into the car.
They were in a hurry now.

Danny hated the taste
of the rubbish.
'Mum!' he mumbled.

**'I'm going to be sick!'**

Mum took Danny
back into the house.
'Bleeaaugh!' went Danny.
He spat all the rubbish
down the toilet.

Mum wiped his mouth.
'You'll need to have something
in case you get sick
in the car,' she said.
She looked around
the bathroom.
Then she gave Danny
**Susie's pink potty**!

At last, they drove away.
Danny was very cross.
He held Susie's potty
on his knee.
He made faces at Susie.

But Susie just smiled.
'Susie teddy!
Danny potty!'
she said.

Soon they arrived
at Auntie Bessie's house.
The kitchen was full of smells.

'Yuck,' said Danny.
He felt very sick.

'Danny!' cried Auntie Bessie.
'You look as green
as my cabbage!'

'Poor Danny is not well,'
said Mum.
'He won't be able to eat
any dinner.'

Auntie Bessie was
chopping the cabbage.
'What a pity!' she said.

But Danny was delighted.
No dinner! he thought.
My trick is working!

Uncle Tom showed Danny
his vegetable patch.

'I have a little present for you,
Danny,' he said.
'I'll give it to you
when you're going home.'

Later, Danny went
into the kitchen.
Auntie Bessie was stirring
the cabbage.

'I have something for you,
Danny!' she said.
'I'll give it to you
when you're going home.'

Danny was having
a great time.
While everyone was eating
dinner, he watched television.
'What a great sick trick!'
he giggled.

'Time for
**chocolate cake**!'
said Auntie Bessie.

'Yippee!' yelled Danny.
'I love chocolate cake!'

Auntie Besse's chocolate cake was **huge**.

The top was covered in
chocolate icing
and there was more
chocolate icing in the middle.
Danny's mouth was watering.

Auntie Bessie cut
a huge slice for Mum.
She cut a huge slice for Dad.
She cut a huge slice
for Uncle Tom.
She even cut a huge slice
for Susie!

'What about **me**?'
said Danny.

Dad slowly licked his lips.
'Sick boys can't eat
chocolate cake,' he said.

Danny was shocked.
But he smiled sweetly
at Auntie Bessie.

She'll keep a slice for me,
he thought.
I know she will!

Soon it was time to go home.
Auntie Bessie gave Danny
a plate covered in tinfoil.
'Take this, dear,' she said.
'You might feel like it
later on.'

Danny hugged her tightly.

'Thanks,' he said.

'You're the best!'

Then Uncle Tom
gave Danny a big bag.
He winked.
'It's for tomorrow,'
he said.

'More chocolate cake!'
cried Danny.
'Yum! **Yum**! **Yum**!'

Danny peeped into the bag.
He saw a caterpillar
crawling on a green leaf.
'**Cabbage**!' he yelled.

Then Danny lifted the tinfoil
on the plate.
'**Dinner**!' he screamed.

There was no chocolate cake.
Danny was very cross.

'Here comes Susie,' said Mum.
'She's got something
for you too, Danny!'

'Danny potty!' said Susie.
She threw her potty at Danny.

Danny walked slowly
to the car.
He was carrying
the dinner plate,
the bag of cabbage
and Susie's pink potty.

'That was a stupid sick trick,'
Danny said. 'I'll never do
anything like it again.
Never. Never. Never.'

But I think he will, don't you?
Danny's just that kind of kid.